中国传统故事美绘本（中英文双语版）

盘古开天

Pangu Creates the World

传说在遥远的太古时期，整个宇宙就像一个大鸡蛋，里面混沌一团，漆黑一片，什么也看不见。没有天，没有地，也没有东西南北，更别说河流山川、花草树木了。但在这个大"鸡蛋"里，孕育着一个伟大的英雄，他就是盘古。

It is said that in the beginning of time the universe was like a cosmic egg. Within it there was no light, no sky, no earth, no rivers, no mountains, and no plants—nothing except a formless chaos. However, in the egg lay a great hero named Pangu.

盘古一直在"鸡蛋"里睡觉,转眼一万八千年过去了。有一天他终于苏醒了,他睁开眼睛,发现周围一片黑暗,看不到一点亮光。可能因为在"鸡蛋"里蜷得太久了,盘古想舒展一下筋骨,然而"鸡蛋"紧紧包裹着他的身体,他连呼吸都困难,别说伸展腿脚了。

他实在无法忍受这样的处境,心想,得想个办法打碎这个"蛋壳"才行。盘古使劲挥舞着拳头,捶打四周坚硬的四壁,但是四壁丝毫不动。四处找不到可以利用的工具,盘古就拔下自己的一颗牙齿,把它变成了一把锋利的神斧,使出浑身力气,向周围砍去。

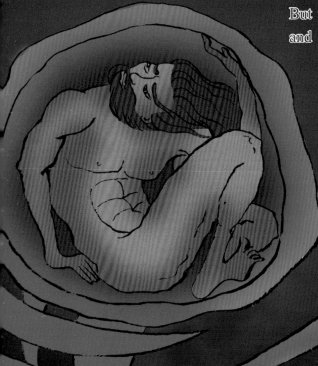

For Pangu, who had slept inside the egg for 18,000 years, the passing time was as but a moment. But then one day he finally woke up and saw the bleak, dark emptiness of the universe. Having lain inside all curled up for too long, Pangu wanted to limber up his muscles and joints, but the egg held him too tightly; he was nearly suffocated, let alone able to stretch out his limbs.

He really could not stand such a predicament and decided that he had to do something to break the egg shell. Pangu beat furiously on the hard shell with his fist, but it remained intact. Since no tools were available around him, Pangu pulled out a tooth from his mouth and turned it into a sharp broad axe, chopping round about him with all his strength.

劈里啪啦一阵巨响过后,"鸡蛋"终于裂开了。只见那些轻而清的东西,飘飘悠悠地,直升到高处,变成了天空;而那些重而浊的东西,则向下沉,形成了大地。这样,宇宙再也不是混沌一片,有了天,有了地,有了光亮。盘古开辟了天地,创造了一个新的世界,十分高兴。

Bang! Bang! After a spell of tremendous noise, the eggshell finally cracked. That which had filled the egg seeped and floated slowly out of the crack. That part of it which was light and pure rose to become the sky and the heavy and muddy part sank to form the earth. The universe was no longer a formless chaos; there emerged the sky, the earth, and light. Pangu was immensely delighted to see this new world.

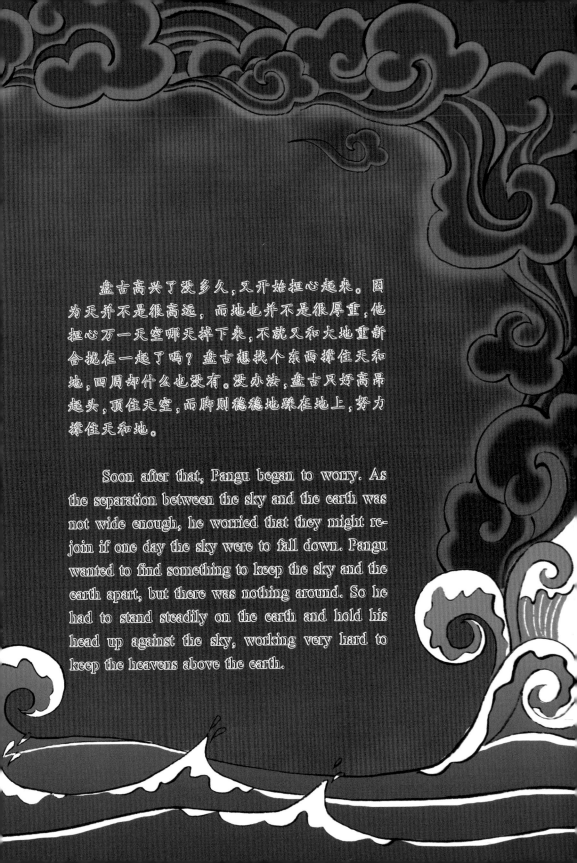

盘古高兴了没多久,又开始担心起来。因为天并不是很高远, 而地也并不是很厚重,他担心万一天空哪天掉下来,不就又和大地重新合拢在一起了吗? 盘古想找个东西撑住天和地,四周却什么也没有。没办法,盘古只好高昂起头,顶住天空,而脚则稳稳地踩在地上,努力撑住天和地。

Soon after that, Pangu began to worry. As the separation between the sky and the earth was not wide enough, he worried that they might rejoin if one day the sky were to fall down. Pangu wanted to find something to keep the sky and the earth apart, but there was nothing around. So he had to stand steadily on the earth and hold his head up against the sky, working very hard to keep the heavens above the earth.

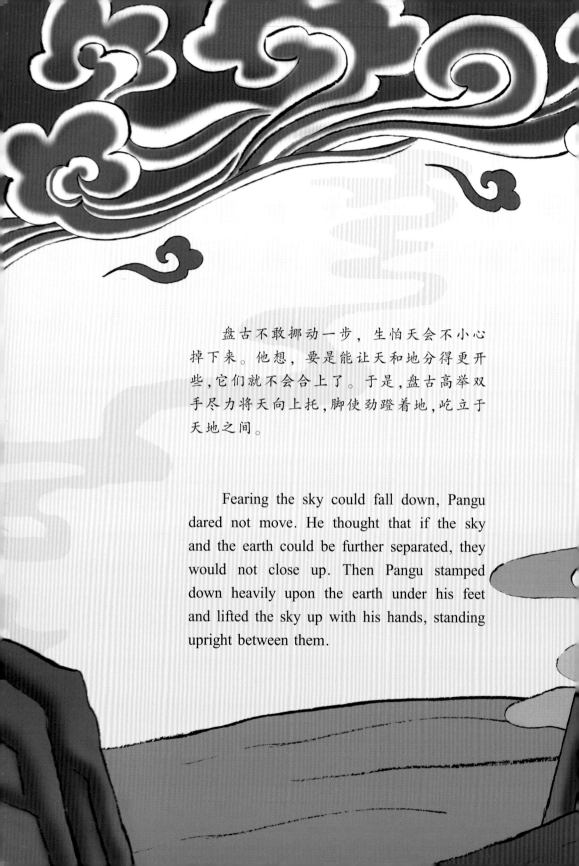

盘古不敢挪动一步，生怕天会不小心掉下来。他想，要是能让天和地分得更开些，它们就不会合上了。于是，盘古高举双手尽力将天向上托，脚使劲蹬着地，屹立于天地之间。

Fearing the sky could fall down, Pangu dared not move. He thought that if the sky and the earth could be further separated, they would not close up. Then Pangu stamped down heavily upon the earth under his feet and lifted the sky up with his hands, standing upright between them.

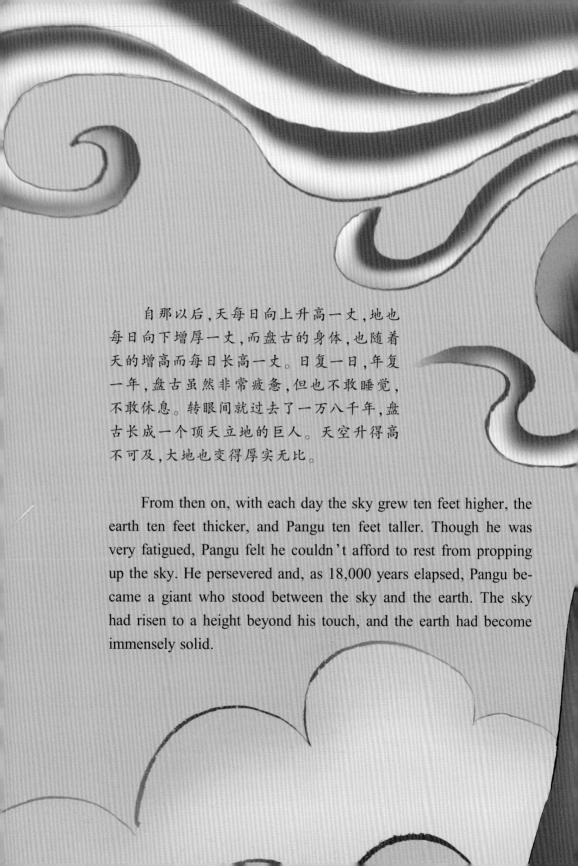

　　自那以后，天每日向上升高一丈，地也每日向下增厚一丈，而盘古的身体，也随着天的增高而每日长高一丈。日复一日，年复一年，盘古虽然非常疲惫，但也不敢睡觉，不敢休息。转眼间就过去了一万八千年，盘古长成一个顶天立地的巨人。天空升得高不可及，大地也变得厚实无比。

From then on, with each day the sky grew ten feet higher, the earth ten feet thicker, and Pangu ten feet taller. Though he was very fatigued, Pangu felt he couldn't afford to rest from propping up the sky. He persevered and, as 18,000 years elapsed, Pangu became a giant who stood between the sky and the earth. The sky had risen to a height beyond his touch, and the earth had become immensely solid.

终于，天不再升高，地也不再增厚，天稳地固，再也不用担心天会塌下来了。盘古这才放下心来，但他也耗尽了所有的力气，累倒在地上。临死前，他依依不舍地看着他开辟的崭新的世界，心想，就把自己的身体也奉献给这个世界吧。

At last, the sky stopped rising and the earth stopped growing. With both in a stable condition, there was no need to worry that the sky might fall. Finally Pangu felt relieved, but he had exhausted all of his energy as well and lay wearily on the ground. Before he died, he reluctantly looked at his newly-created world and decided that his whole body should also be left to the world.

　　于是盘古临死前呼出的气息，变成了流动的风和飘动的云；他发出的声音，化作了天空中隆隆的雷声。

　　盘古的头化作了东山，他的脚化作了西山，他的左臂化作了南山，他的右臂化作了北山，他的肚子化作了中山。这五座山雄伟壮丽，直插云霄，就像五根巨大的擎天柱支撑着辽阔的天空。

His breath became the wind and the clouds, his voice the thunder. His head formed the Eastern Mountain, his feet the Western Mountain, his left arm the Southern Mountain, his right arm the Northern Mountain, and his belly the Central Mountain. The five mountains were extremely high and grand, just like five huge pillars supporting the sky.

　　盘古的左眼变成了灿烂的太阳,照耀大地,给世界带来了光明和温暖,使万物生长;他的右眼变成了皎洁的月亮,给夜晚带来光明,照亮了夜晚的大地;他的头发变成了夜空中闪烁的颗颗繁星,点缀着美丽的夜空。

　　Pangu's left eye became the sun which shines on the earth giving light and heat to the world and making all things on the earth grow. His right eye became the moon which illuminates the nighttime earth. His hair formed the twinkling stars, spangling the beautiful night sky.

盘古的鲜血化作了江河湖海，日夜奔流不息；他的肌肤，化作了辽阔的大地，带给万物生存的养分；他的筋脉变成了一条条纵横交错的道路，通向遥远的地方。

Pangu's blood formed rivers, flowing day and night; his skin and muscles the fertile lands, bringing nutrients to all plants; his veins a criss-cross of roads, leading to remote places.

盘古的汗毛，变成了茂盛的花草树木，装扮着生机勃勃的世界；他的汗水，变成了雨露，滋润万物；他的骨头牙齿，化作了玉石金属，供人们观赏使用。

从此，天上有了日月星辰，地上有了山川树木、鸟兽虫鱼。盘古用尽他所有的力气和他的整个身体，创造了一个无比美丽的世界。

Pangu's fur became the bushes and forests, dressing up a dynamic world; his sweat fell as rain, moistening all things on the earth; his bones and teeth were now the valuable minerals and metals, for people to see and use.

From that time on, there have been the sun, the moon and the stars in the sky; the earth has been filled with mountains, rivers, birds, beasts, insects and fish. Using his body and all of his strength, Pangu created a magnificent world.

完

End